A Note to Parents and Teachers

Dorling Kindersley Readers is a compelling new reading programme for children, designed in conjunction with leading literacy experts, including Cliff Moon M.Ed., Honorary Fellow of the University of Reading. Cliff Moon has spent many years as a teacher and teacher educator specializing in reading and has written more than 140 books for children and teachers. He reviews regularly for teachers' journals.

Beautiful illustrations and superb full-colour photographs combine with engaging, easy-to-read stories to offer a fresh approach to each subject in the series. Each *Dorling Kindersley Reader* is guaranteed to capture a child's interest while developing his or her reading skills, general knowledge, and love of reading.

The four levels of *Dorling Kindersley Readers* are aimed at different reading abilities, enabling you to choose the books that are exactly right for your child:

Level 1 – Beginning to read
Level 2 – Beginning to read alone
Level 3 – Reading alone
Level 4 – Proficient readers

The "normal" age at which a child begins to read can be anywhere from three to eight years old, so these levels are intended only as a general guideline.

No matter which level you select, you can be sure that you are helping children learn to read, then read to learn!

Dorling  Kindersley

LONDON, NEW YORK, MUNICH, PARIS
MELBOURNE, DELHI

Project Editor Deborah Murrell
Art Editor Catherine Goldsmith
Senior Art Editor Sarah Ponder
Managing Editor Bridget Gibbs
Senior DTP Designer Bridget Roseberry
Production Melanie Dowland
Picture Researcher Frances Vargo
Picture Librarian Sally Hamilton
Jacket Designer Margherita Gianni

Reading Consultant
Cliff Moon, M.Ed.

Published in Great Britain by
Dorling Kindersley Limited
80 The Strand, London WC2R 0RL
A Penguin Company

4 6 8 10 9 7 5 3

A CIP catalogue record for this book is
available from the British Library.

ISBN 0-7513-2139-7

Color reproduction by Colourscan, Singapore
Printed and bound in China by L Rex

The publisher would like to thank the following:
Photography: Dave King, John Downs 14
Illustrations: Simone Boni/L.R. Galante
Natural History Museum: 8-9, 11, 12-13, 14, 15, 21
Ardea London Ltd.: Arthur Hayward 16-17

see our complete
catalogue at

www.dk.com

DORLING KINDERSLEY *READERS*

BEGINNING 1 TO READ

Dinosaur's Day

Written by Ruth Thomson

DK

A Dorling Kindersley Book

I am Triceratops.
I am a dinosaur and
I am big and strong.

Triceratops
(try-SER-uh-tops)

I have three spiky horns
on my head and
I have a bony frill
on my neck.

frill

I look fierce but
I am quite gentle.

beak

I spend all day eating plants.
I snip off twigs and leaves
with my hard beak.

I live in a group
called a herd.
We keep watch
for fierce dinosaurs because
they might want to eat us!

All sorts of other dinosaurs
live near the river with us.

Everything is peaceful.

All of a sudden,
what do I see?

A Tyrannosaurus!
He is the fiercest dinosaur of all.

Tyrannosaurus
(tie-RAN-uh-SORE-us)

He has strong toes
and sharp claws.
He has a huge mouth
full of sharp teeth.

toes

A herd of shy dinosaurs
spots Tyrannosaurus too.
They run away on their long legs
as fast as they can.
They will hide in the forest.

Ornithomimus
(OR-ni-thoh-MEE-mus)

These duck-billed dinosaurs
stop eating.
They watch Tyrannosaurus.
If he comes too close,
they will run away too.

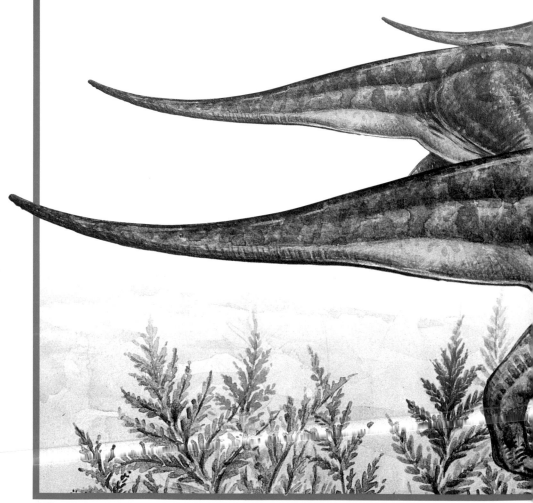

bill

Edmontosaurus
(ed-MON-tuh-SORE-us)

This bone-headed dinosaur
looks up and sniffs the air.
He can smell Tyrannosaurus.
If Tyrannosaurus
comes too close,
he will also run away.

Pachycephalosaurus
(PAK-ee-SEF-uh-low-SORE-us)

The dinosaurs with crests
hoot in alarm.

crest

Parasaurolophus
(par-uh-sore-OLL-uh-fuss)

The armoured dinosaur has a club
on the end of his tail.
He gets ready to swing it
at Tyrannosaurus.

club

Ankylosaurus
(an-KIE-luh-SORE-us)

I am busy watching
all the other dinosaurs and
I forget to stay with my herd.

I can see Tyrannosaurus and
he can see me.

Tyrannosaurus runs towards me.
He looks hungry and
his eyes are glinting.

teeth

His mouth is open and
I can see his sharp teeth.

Thud!
Thud!

He comes nearer
and nearer...

Tyrannosaurus
stands up.
He is very tall.
He lifts his head
and roars loudly.

Tyrannosaurus is trying
to frighten me but
I am not scared.
I have my pointed horns
for fighting and
I have my bony frill
to protect me.

I lower my head and
bellow loudly.
Ready, set,
here I come!
Perhaps I can stab
Tyrannosaurus
with my spiky horns.

horns

Tyrannosaurus tries to bite me
with his sharp teeth.
I am still not scared.
I kick up the dust and
try to stab him.

Tyrannosaurus is getting tired.
He stops fighting and turns away.
He goes to look for
a smaller dinosaur
for his dinner.

Now I am safe and
I am going to look for my herd.
I am very hungry
after all that fighting.

I am glad to be back
with my herd
by the river.

The other dinosaurs come back
to the river as well.
They start eating peacefully.

I hope Tyrannosaurus
won't come back again!

31

Picture word list

frill

page 5

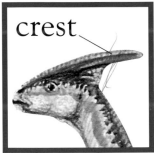

crest

page 15

beak

page 6

club

page 17

toes

page 10

teeth

page 20

bill

page 13

horns

page 25